Chelonia Green
Champion *of* Turtles

Christobel Mattingley

ALLEN&UNWIN

First published in 2008

Allen & Unwin
83 Alexander St
Crows Nest NSW 2065
Australia
Phone: (61 2) 8425 0100
Fax: (61 2) 9906 2218
Email: info@allenandunwin.com
Web: www.allenandunwin.com

National Library of Australia
Cataloguing-in-Publication entry:

Mattingley, Christobel, 1931–
Chelonia green, champion of turtles

ISBN: 978 174175 171 0 (pbk.)

For children.

Sea turtles--Queensland--Juvenile fiction.
Wildlife rescue--Juvenile fiction.
Conservation of natural resources –Juvenile fiction.

A823.4

Cover and text design by Zoe Sadokierski
Set in 12/18pt pt Abode Garamond Pro by Midland Typesetters, Australia.
Printed in Australia by McPherson's Printing Group

10 9 8 7 6 5 4 3 2 1

Teachers' notes available from www.allenandunwin.com

To Nina, Chris and
Bethwynne

With grateful memories of Miss Knox,
my headmistress, who berated the whole school
at assembly if she found so much as a piece of
orange peel in the grounds

Contents

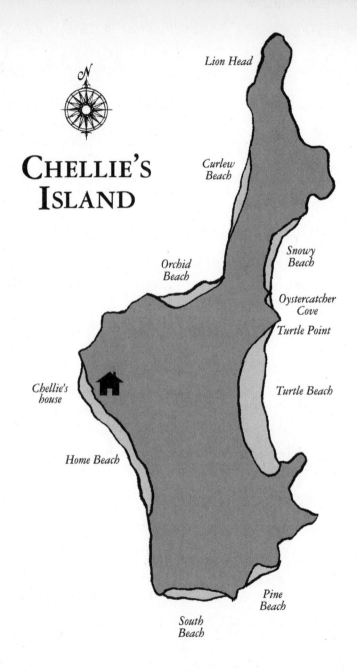

CHELLIE'S
ISLAND

Lion Head

Curlew
Beach

Snowy
Beach

Orchid
Beach

Oystercatcher
Cove

Turtle Point

Chellie's
house

Turtle Beach

Home Beach

Pine
Beach

South
Beach

CHAPTER I
Chelonia Green

CHELONIA GREEN WAS NOT HER real name. Although she wished it was. She had made it up herself.

When her mother called, 'Michelle, where are you?' she often didn't hear.

When her mother called, 'Michelle Braddon, where *are* you?' she never heard.

But when her father called, 'Chellie, where are you?' she always heard. And ran to meet him.

It wasn't that she did not love her mum as much as she loved her dad. But Mum was usually calling her to come and do her lessons. While Dad would probably say, 'How about some beachcombing?' Or if the tide was right, 'Shall we go and see the turtles?'

Even though Mum was a good teacher and made lessons interesting, why would you want to sit inside when you could wander along the beach with Dad, who knew so much about everything on the island? When you might find all sorts of treasures at high tide, and, best of all, see turtles at low tide in the big rock pool.

Chellie could remember the very first time Dad had taken her to see the turtles, just after the family came to live on the island. Her little legs had been so short that Dad had carried her piggyback through the long grass down the sandhills. He had lifted her over the spiny trunks of fallen pandanus trees and swung her down over the edge of the sandbank. Onto the longest, widest, most beautiful beach Chellie had ever seen in her life.

The sea was bluer than the sky. The foam was whiter than the clouds.

'Look at all the white horses!' Dad pointed to the flying spray streaming from the big green waves rolling towards them.

Chellie smelled their saltiness and tasted it on her lips. She scampered along the beach beside Dad, who was heading towards a big outcrop of rocks. All jumbled together, the rocks were – dark as prunes, brown as raisins, golden as sultanas. They looked like a huge fruitcake, the sort she liked to help Mum mix. Dad picked Chellie up again and carried her over big rocks and drifts of smaller rocks, and put her down to run along the strips of buttery yellow sand in between. He carried her again over the last steep ridge and sat her on his shoulders to look down.

There in the shimmering green water below lay four big oval shapes. Chellie thought they looked like a giant's carving dishes. They were patterned in brownish green and had five handles. Suddenly the handles stirred, and the giant's carving dishes began to move!

Upward – backward, forward – downward went one pair of handles, while the other smaller handles stayed steady. The fifth handle poked up above the water and looked at Chellie with heavy-lidded eyes.

Chellie pummelled Dad's head in excitement. 'What are they?'

'Turtles,' Dad said.

'Turtles,' Chellie repeated. 'Turtles.' What a lovely word. She rolled it around in her mouth. Turtles. Turtles. Turtles.

'Green turtles. *Chelonia* is their scientific name.'

Chellie loved the big words, like *scientific*, that Dad used. And she thought that Chelonia was the most beautiful word she had ever heard. She whispered it to herself. Chelonia. Chelonia. And green. Green was her favourite colour. She would be Chelonia Green.

Chapter 2
Beaches

CHELLIE WAS OLDER NOW AND much bigger. Her legs were longer, stronger. She roamed the island from side to side, from end to end. She explored the bushy gullies where fruit bats hung in the trees like black umbrellas, furling and unfurling their wings. She climbed the hummocky hills to survey the sea and the surrounding islands, looking for whales in winter and spring. She circled the dam to watch the swallows skimming its brown surface, and the rainbow birds flashing down to drink.

Best of all, Chellie loved the beaches. The island had eight – one for each day of the week and one to spare, Dad joked. Depending on the way the wind was blowing, Chellie decided which one to visit.

The west beach was Home Beach, where Dad usually brought in the boat to unload stores. It was long and sloping, with deep soft sand the colour of caramel, and sticky too. The sand coated Chellie's feet in glittering socks of shell grit. Home Beach was the best beach of all for shells. Twice a day the tide left a ripple of them at high-water mark, and Chellie wandered along looking for limpets, whelks, cockles, cowries and fragments of bright red coral.

Around the rocky headland at South Beach the sand was different. Softer, finer, silky, silvery. It was Chellie's favourite swimming place.

Mum always said, 'Don't go out over your depth,' and although Chellie sometimes wanted to, she never did. Chellie knew the glistening green water was home to many creatures, some of them much bigger than she was. She was lucky to share it with them. It was fun to pretend she was a fish darting, or a dolphin leaping, or a ray slowly flapping.

The southwest beach was called Pine Beach

because of the hoop pines which grew among its craggy cliffs. A lot of flotsam and jetsam washed up here, and Chellie liked fossicking in the drifts by the sandbanks. You never knew what you might find.

On the other side of the island, the sight of the long sweeping curve of Turtle Beach still made Chellie draw in her breath every time she breasted its sheltering sandhills. If an easterly were blowing, the sea would send in long slow rollers frilled with foam. Then Dad and Chellie would go body surfing.

'Exhilarating!' Dad would shout, with the foam clinging in a white curl to his wet hair.

Turtle Point and the oyster-encrusted rocks beyond hugged a smaller beach. At low tide a pair of oystercatchers probed just above the water line with their long red bills, their reflections shining in the wet sand. Chellie wondered how they managed to break open the ridged, purple oyster shells, but the many empty white shells on the rocks proved they did.

Beyond Oystercatcher Cove, it was time for rock-hopping. Dad had shown Chellie how to recognise the different sorts of rocks – sedimentary, metamorphic, igneous. Chellie repeated their names as she scrambled and clambered and jumped from outcrop to outcrop –

over fallen slabs of cliff, past caves and blow holes, along thick seams of white and yellow quartz like neglected teeth.

At last the long straight stretch of the northeast beach appeared beyond the rocks – white, dazzling white. It was the only white beach on the island. Chellie had never seen snow, but she was sure it couldn't look any whiter than this sand. So she called it Snowy Beach.

On again, more rocks to climb to the northernmost point of the island – a rugged headland jutting fiercely out into the sea. From the boat it looked like a crouching lion, so she called it Lion Head.

Round the corner, past Lion Head, stretched another beach. The north beach. Not quite as white as Snowy Beach, but beautiful too, printed with the three-toed tracks of curlews like little arrows. When Chellie came across a curlew, it always gave her a start. Its sand-coloured plumage made it blend into the background, and it stood so still that it looked like a piece of driftwood.

'Camouflage,' Dad said. But Chellie could see its eyes watching her and would back away. After all, it was the curlews' place more than hers. Curlew Beach.

Yet another stretch of rocks, honeycombed and sculpted into the weirdest shapes by sea and wind, had to be crossed to reach the northwest beach. Here the reef was close inshore, and the beach disappeared at high tide. But orchids with little green and yellow flowers like butterflies, the only orchids on the island, clung in crevices in the cliff face. So it was Orchid Beach.

Past another rocky point caressed by casuarinas, Chellie was back to where she had started. Home Beach.

Chapter 3
The Turtles

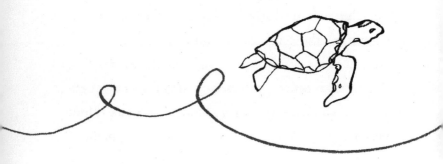

CHELLIE DID HER LESSONS WITH the School of Distance Education. Each month when Dad went to the mainland to collect the stores, he picked up a fat package addressed to *Michelle Braddon, C/o the Post Office*. Chellie liked opening her mail and looking over all the material she would study with Mum through the next four weeks. She and Mum eagerly checked what her other teacher, Miss Howe, had written on the assignments they had sent in last time. When it was *Good work, Michelle*, or *Well done*, they were both pleased.

'Let's make a cake,' Mum would say, and the maths lesson for the day would be weighing and measuring the ingredients, calculating quantities and cooking time. Chellie liked helping to make bread too. The smell of it baking as she did her worksheets was one of the best smells she knew.

For a break she would help hang out the washing, pegging tea towels, pillowcases and knickers tight against the tugging wind. Or she weeded the carrots or picked the peas. When the chooks clucked triumphantly, Chellie would hurry out to hunt for their eggs among the tussocky grass and under the lime tree, before the crows could get them.

Then it didn't seem long before Mum announced, 'Okay. School's finished for today.'

Chellie would be off at once – a sandwich in one pocket, an orange in the other. Off to visit the turtles if the tide was falling. Over the hummocky hills, through the wind-shorn bush, onto the sandhills, down to the beach. Running, laughing, somersaulting, skipping, splashing through the dancing waves, shouting to the turtles, 'I'm coming, I'm coming.'

She was as nimble and sure-footed as the goats on the island across the water. She jumped easily from rock to rock, across the crevices and gulches and rock pools where crabs clicked and scuttled sideways out of sight. The grey heron flapped into the air at her coming, and the oystercatcher out on the point where the waves were breaking piped a shrill alarm.

'Silly bird,' Chellie chided. 'You know I'll never hurt you.'

Lightly, she made her way up onto the ridge that overlooked the big pool where the turtles rested, wondering how many and which ones would be there. Sometimes there were seven, sometimes eight or nine or ten. Fourteen was the most she had ever seen. She was quiet now, as quiet as the turtles, squatting to count them. They were aware of her presence but did not move. Chellie was sure they knew her, knew that she was their friend.

Each turtle seemed to have a favourite place: resting half out of the water on a shallow ledge, or floating in the sun in the middle of the pool, or sleeping in the shadow of an overhanging slab. Chellie pondered each elegantly patterned, curved carapace, and marvelled at the way the leathery mosaic on the flippers, neck and head matched the hard shell. The mottles all merged into the dimples and dapples of the water, so that even such a large creature became difficult to distinguish when it submerged.

When one turtle stirred and began to swim, others followed. Chellie was rapt. Absorbed in watching their graceful movements, she did not feel the hard rock under her bottom, and totally forgot the sandwich in her pocket. All she knew was the slow rhythm of the turtle ballet.

The three biggest were each over a metre long. 'They could be more than sixty years old,' Dad had told her. Chellie marvelled. Twice as old as Mum and Dad. As old as her gran.

Dad called the biggest The Dowager. 'She's a matriarch and still laying eggs.'

It was awesome. Chellie tried to imagine Gran having babies, but couldn't.

One turtle had a damaged shell. 'Run over by a boat,' Dad said sadly. Chellie called her Scarback. Another had a nick out of its shell, so became Nicky.

Flip's back left flipper was missing, and Flop's back right flipper was gone. 'Probably grabbed by a shark. Or chopped by a propeller,' Dad surmised.

Chellie shuddered.

'Hard work for them when they have to cover their eggs. They use their front ones to dig the nest, but only their hind ones to backfill,' Dad explained.

Most of the turtles were females. Ladies-in-waiting was Dad's name for them. Waiting for the time when they would lay their eggs.

The males had much bigger tails and were more restless. Mostly they swam underwater, just popping their heads up from time to time to breathe. Sometimes it was not the male turtles that disturbed the peace of the pool. Other creatures lived there too. A fierce, long streak of a fish would dart out from under the seaweedy rock in the centre to chase the little fish, which flashed and skimmed in a glittering cloud. They would peel off into two smaller clouds to try to elude the predator pursuing them into the deep shadow.

Chellie moved quietly around the main pool, pausing beside each turtle at the edge. Then she went to check the smaller pools beyond, where other turtles might be resting. Sometimes a loggerhead turtle was in the furthest outlying pool. It seemed to know it was not part of the green family and kept apart. It had a different pattern of scales on its reddish brown shell, and its head was much bigger and chunkier, with a mouth that could crunch shellfish, crabs, sea urchins and jellyfish.

'Not like the greens. They're vegetarians,' Dad joked.

'What's its scientific name?' Chellie had asked.

'*Caretta caretta*,' Dad replied.

'Caretta,' Chellie repeated. 'I like that.' So Caretta it was, and this turtle became Chellie's favourite.

When the tide turned and water began rising in the pools, swirling through the seaward channels, bubbling up through the crevices, Chellie knew it was time to leave.

'Goodbye, turtles,' she whispered.

If the tide was already rising when she reached the sandhills, she would settle in a little hollow out of the wind and gaze at Turtle Point disappearing under the waves. Chellie loved to think of the turtles moving out to feed, swimming free in the deep sea, which held no secrets for them.

But there *were* secrets right where she sat. Many years ago, Aboriginal people had sat in this very same sheltered hollow, talking and laughing where now only the wind in the casuarinas sighed a slow lament. Chellie sifted through her fingers the fragments of purple shells from their feasts, imagining women gathering oysters from the rocks below, while children played on the beach.

In her mind's eye she could see men too, squatting here, patiently chipping implements out of stones from the shingle at the foot of the cliffs. She picked up spearheads, marvelling at the sharpness of the flaked blades, and discovered heavy hammers shaped to fit snugly in the hand. Perhaps the men had hunted turtles too, lighting a fire of driftwood on the beach to cook their catch. Surely they would have come in the nesting season, so that the women could gather turtle eggs.

Chapter 4
Nesting

CHELLIE AND HER PARENTS WATCHED eagerly for nesting turtles. Chellie knew that turtles, like so many other creatures, are under threat of extinction because of changes in their habitat, both on land and at sea.

'The turtles that nest on our island are lucky,' Dad commented. 'No foxes. No dogs or feral pigs to sniff out the nests and eat the eggs, the way they do on so many mainland beaches. No foreshore developments encroaching on the coast, and no lights to confuse the turtles.'

Chellie giggled at the thought of their island's foreshore developments: a sandy track for the tractor to pull the boat out of the water and two little solar lamps, which Dad always removed at the beginning of the nesting season. He didn't replace the lamps until months later, after the last hatchlings had emerged. But Chellie knew that there were plenty of other risks facing the baby turtles. Before they even reached the water, predatory crabs and sea birds waited. And in the sea beyond, hungry fish hunted these bite-sized snacks.

From late November through the summer, Chellie went out each evening with her parents to look for nesting turtles. No torches, no talking. Home Beach was the turtles' favourite because of its soft deep sand. They liked high tide and seemed to prefer a full moon or a new moon. Chellie loved wandering along in the moonlight, listening to the lapping of the waves, watching for a dark shape to emerge from the water.

Sometimes, even though they stood still and silent, the turtle seemed to sense they were there and would turn and lumber back into the water. But usually she continued on her heavy way until she found a place for her precious burden of eggs. Chellie could hear the scrape scrape scrape as, with all four flippers working steadily, the turtle would send loose sand flying to clear a pit for her body. Half an hour it usually took, with the Southern Cross moving slowly slowly in the deep blue above.

Then she might pause a little before starting to dig a deep egg chamber with her hind flippers. That took at least another quarter of an hour. Nearly an hour of silent watching since the turtle had left the water. But although Chellie had seen it many times now, she grew so absorbed in the wonder of it, that she didn't feel the pins and needles in her legs.

Dad might shine a carefully shaded torch, just for a moment, and Chellie would catch her breath at the gleam of eggs like ping-pong balls dropping into their chamber. Minutes later it was over, and the sand would fly again as the turtle began covering her nest. This could take as long as it had to dig it and Chellie counted stars again – the Southern Cross and the Saucepan, which Dad called Orion's Belt. But she could never even begin to count the myriad myriad twinkles in the Milky Way.

The moon rode higher and higher in the mysterious night sky. At last the mother turtle was satisfied she had done her best. She lumbered back down the beach to the welcoming water, leaving her eggs to hatch by themselves six weeks later in the warmth of the sand.

Chellie let out a sigh as the dark shape disappeared into the sea, and she wondered if she would ever see it again. Turtles do come back to the same beach to nest all through their long lives, she knew. But they don't breed every year, so it could be two or five or even eight years before this green turtle returned. She might be setting off on a migration back to her usual feeding grounds, which could be up to 3000 kilometres away in the Pacific Ocean. Chellie felt dazed, amazed, astonished that a creature which could be as old as her grandma, even as her great-grandma, could still produce babies, and still swim all that way. Turtles truly are awesome creatures, she decided.

She stumbled a bit as they walked back, so Mum and Dad gave her a chairlift home. Then it was time for a warm Milo and a biscuit before Mum tucked her into bed. After turtle-watching nights, Chellie dreamed watery green turtle dreams and woke late. Lucky that nesting time was during school holidays.

Chapter 5
Hatching!

EVEN MORE EXCITING THAN WATCHING the mother turtles lay eggs was watching the baby turtles emerge. Dad and Chellie kept a record of all the nests and the dates they had been made, so they had a good idea when and where to look for hatchlings.

Chellie had read that breaking through the leathery shell took a baby turtle up to twenty-four hours. The baby had to uncurl and straighten out and eat the rest of its egg yolk to give it strength to climb up to the surface. The little turtles waited until all were ready to make the big push up through the sand, breathing air between the grains as they climbed. That marathon could take several days.

As if they sensed there was safety in numbers, one hundred and more broke through the surface together, usually at night. Chellie loved the sight of them hurrying, scurrying across the sand, flippers moving like dog paddle, down towards the sea they had never seen. They were so tiny. So cute. She longed to pick them up and help them on their way. Their little shells were smaller than the palm of her hand. It was hard to imagine that they could grow into something as large and as heavy as The Dowager.

Sadly, most of them probably never would. The rush down the beach was only the first of many dangers the young turtles faced. Once they reached the water they were in a cold harsh world where they were easy prey for sharks, fish and diving birds. Perhaps one in a thousand might survive all the hazards to return thirty years later as an adult.

'Go, little turtles, go!' Chellie breathed. 'Stay safe, stay strong, grow, grow, grow. And come back again. Please do!'

Chapter 6
Caretta

AFTER THE LATEST HATCHING, the sun was well up when Chellie woke. She jumped out of bed and hastily pulled on shorts and top, determined not to waste another moment of the beautiful blue day. Dad and Mum had already had breakfast. Chellie could hear the sound of the tractor over near the dam and could see Mum's big sun hat bobbing among the tomato bushes. She chomped through her muesli, downed her milk and ran out into the hot January morning.

Waving to her mother, she called over her shoulder, 'Tide's right for Turtle Point. See ya!'

She raced towards the track, singing a song to encourage the hatchlings as she ran. 'Sharks stay away, today and every day, from the baby turtles out in the bay. Noddies and boobies stay away, today and every day, from the baby turtles out in the bay. Hungry fish stay away, today and every day, from the baby turtles out in the bay.'

Over the hummocks she panted, pausing at last for breath on the sandhill. She never grew tired of that special moment when she looked down on the shining expanse of sand and sea that was Turtle Beach. So strong, so wild, so free. Chellie felt a thrill every time.

But today the thrill turned to chill. She shivered. Her heart seemed to drop into her guts like a big black lump. Like the big black lump dumped by the receding tide, a blot on the mirror-bright sand.

A great knot of seaweed? A hunk of wood?

Not a turtle, Chellie told herself. A turtle wouldn't come ashore on a falling tide in bright sunlight. They rarely nested here anyway, because the sand was so hard. And there were no tracks leading down from the narrow strip of soft sand above high-tide mark.

A couple of circling gulls swooped in and began to peck at the still, dark form.

'No! No!' Chellie shouted, waving her arms frantically.

She flung herself down the slope, heedless of hidden hollows, scratching bushes and sly, long runners of marram grass waiting to trip her and send her tumbling. She pushed through the rattling pandanus and jumped off the bank down to the beach.

More gulls had joined the first two. Chellie felt the muesli and milk rising in her throat as she ran towards the water's edge. It can't be a turtle. It mustn't be a turtle.

But it was.

A big brown turtle. A loggerhead.

'Caretta!' Chellie sobbed.

The gulls took wing, protesting raucously that she had disturbed them before they could begin to feed.

Chellie knelt down beside the big creature. She had never touched Caretta before. Not even when she lay dreaming in her own peaceful rock pool. Now Chellie stroked the red-brown shell and lifted the lifeless flippers gently. She stared in horror at Caretta's sturdy head, enmeshed in a cruel snarl of silvery fishing line.

Fishing line which the turtle must have mistaken for a jellyfish. Fishing line which had choked her. Choked her to death.

The dark eyes that had watched Chellie so many times without fear were dulled. They would never again see the cool green sea light, the shining flash of fish, the wonders of the coral reefs. Those powerful flippers would never again make the long swim to distant Pacific cays. They would never excavate another nesting chamber.

Although the sun was burning the back of her neck and knees, Chellie was cold inside. Cold cold cold. Caretta might have lived another fifty years. Or more. But now she was dead. Dead dead dead.

Tense and stiff, Chellie got to her feet. And began to run. Stumbling at first, then loping more easily up to the bank, pulling herself up, pushing past the pandanus trees, puffing up the hill, then running running running towards the sound of the tractor.

'Dad!' she screamed, long before he could hear her. 'Dad!'

But he saw her and switched off the engine. He jumped down and ran towards her.

'Caretta's dead!' she wailed, flinging herself into his arms.

Chapter 7
The Challenge

DAD GATHERED CHELLIE UP AS if she was a three-year-old again, and set off back the way she had come. She could feel his strong heart beating and his sweat trickling onto her.

He set her down at the top of the sandhills. Together they looked to the beach. The seagulls had returned. Chellie shivered again. Dad took her hand and together they slithered down. She could taste Dad's sweat and her own tears salty on her tongue.

Dad squeezed her hand as they stood silently

looking at Caretta. 'She's dead all right,' he said quietly. 'Done for by that discarded fishing line. Careless beggars fishermen can be sometimes. Don't stop to think before they toss stuff overboard, treating the sea as if it's a garbage tip. And turtles are so vulnerable. Can't tell the difference between fishing line or a plastic bag and a nice juicy jellyfish.'

Chellie felt a surge of anger and a wave of despair.

'Loggerheads are *endangered*!' she wailed. 'And Caretta hasn't even laid her eggs yet. At least, we haven't seen any of her tracks.'

'She may have started, laid at least one clutch somewhere,' Dad tried to comfort her.

But the tears rolled down Chellie's cheeks. 'Caretta could have laid six clutches this season. She could have had 750 babies. And one might have survived.'

They stood a few more long minutes looking at the victim of someone's carelessness.

'Shall we bury her, Dad?'

'No, Chellie. The sea will take care of its own. Nature will see to that.'

'I don't want the gulls eating her. Or the crabs.' Chellie glared up at the wheeling gulls shrieking overhead.

'Gulls are scavengers,' Dad reminded her. 'They do a good job cleaning up.'

Chellie shuddered. 'Can we take a photo of her, Dad? I'll run home for the camera.'

'Good idea,' Dad agreed. 'We can send it to the turtle research people.'

But just as she turned to set off, Mum's hat appeared on the skyline. Then Mum appeared.

'I've brought the camera,' she shouted. 'When I saw you both tear off, I thought it might be something you could want to photograph.' She held out the camera and looked down at the turtle which would never go to sea again. 'Sadly I was right.'

Chellie flung herself into her mother's arms. 'Mum, it's Caretta. And loggerheads are *endangered*.'

Mum held her tight as she sobbed.

After a moment she pulled away and knelt down at Caretta's head. 'Look at this, Mum. She didn't have a chance.'

Dad took a close-up shot of the vicious tangle of fishing line and one of Chellie kneeling beside the dead loggerhead. 'See if you can find a couple of metres of rope or twine up in the sea wrack, and we'll measure her. She doesn't have a tag, so she's not on the research record.'

It didn't take Chellie long to find what Dad had asked for among the seaweed beyond the high-tide mark. Usually she liked combing through all the things that the sea had washed up: a fishing float that Dad could use at the mooring; a long, striped cushion which Mum put on the bench by the back door. Chellie had found coathangers, combs, clothes pegs, and even ballpoint pens that still worked. Once she found a big plastic crate, which Dad took to store things in the shed. Another time she found a perfectly good chopping board, which Mum was pleased to have. A plastic rake head, a paint brush, a broom head, some big plant pots, a swim flipper, a ball and a towel were all treasure trove. She once carried home a bike seat even though she didn't have a bike, and once a square of blue carpet, which Mum laid beside her bed.

But now suddenly she was aware, as never before, of all the lengths of frayed and knotted rope, the ragged swatches of netting, the long strips of vicious plastic binding, the tangles of fishing line – vicious vicious fishing line – and the plastic lures with lethal hooks and barbs. Plastic bags galore. And bottles. Dozens and dozens of plastic bottles: soft drink, sauce, shampoo, detergent. Even poison. Chellie's anger flared again. How could people throw *poison* bottles into the sea?

As Chellie raced back to Dad with the rope for measuring Caretta, she vowed that in future she would pick up every single piece of rubbish that found its way onto the island beaches. Every single piece.

Chapter 8
Storm

Down on the southern horizon dark clouds were forming, moving fast, blotting out the blue sky with sombre grey. Chellie and Dad measured Caretta.

'She's over a metre,' Dad calculated. 'Probably fully grown. A beautiful specimen.'

Chellie nodded, swallowing her tears.

Dad looked up at the rapidly advancing clouds. 'We'd better start moving. They'll be dumping on us before we get home.'

Back up the sandhills. Back through the bush,

where the birds had gone quiet. Along the sandy track, where ants were hurrying with little white eggs. Then the first heavy drops of rain. Slow and soft at first, but becoming thicker, faster, harder, heavier. By the time they reached the porch it was pelting down, gurgling through the gutters into the thirsty tanks.

Chellie's hair hung in dripping strands. Mum's sunhat drooped wetly over her face. Dad was clutching the camera inside his shirt. Chellie peeled off her sodden top and kicked off her squelchy shoes.

Mum hugged her. 'Let's get lunch.'

She made Chellie's favourite salad sandwiches and Chellie squeezed limes for a big jug of squash, which was so refreshing on a hot day.

After lunch, while the casuarinas wept in the rain, Dad and Chellie worked at the computer, writing their report to the turtle research people.

'They'll need to know her measurements, where we found her and what caused her death,' Dad said.

Chellie keyed in Caretta's length and the measurement at the broadest point of her carapace, thinking of her as a hatchling on a summer night – a tiny determined speck of life, heading by instinct to her future home, the sea. It had taken Caretta thirty years or more to grow to this size. She was probably more than three times as old as Chellie. She had known a world Chellie could never know. Those heavy-lidded eyes, which exuded tears to cleanse her body from the salt in the water she drank, would never weep again. But Chellie would.

Dad suggested they put in the longitude and latitude of their island and describe Turtle Beach's position. Then the cause of death. Chellie felt as if the vicious fishing line was caught in her own mouth: cutting, choking, stifling her breathing. Dad patted her on the back.

'Now we'll put in our names and the date. And then we can attach the photos. Lucky we splurged on that digital camera at Christmas. Let's hope the phone connection is working and we can get our email away.'

The rain eased, and after tea Mum and Dad decided to go looking for a nest that was due to send forth its hatchlings. 'Coming?' they asked Chellie.

Chellie shook her head, 'Not tonight.'

She just didn't have the heart. It was all very well to write that report to the research people, but measurements and latitudes did not express how she felt about Caretta. After her parents had left, she took out her pad and wrote at the top of a new sheet – *Caretta's Cruel Death*.

The pain and anger flowed from the tip of her ballpoint across the page. She wrote and wrote, seeing Caretta lying peacefully in her rock pool, seeing her like a ballet dancer in the clear sunlit depths of the sea. Seeing her lifeless on the beach. Choked and starved to death. Seeing a fisherman cutting away a length of line tangled by his carelessness, tossing it overboard as if the sea was just a garbage tip. Seeing all the plastic and rope and twine littering beaches that had been pristine.

At last she had written out her heart's burden. She laid down her pen and put the sheets into her folder. Mum and Dad were not back yet. She wished they were. The air felt still, heavy, ominous. A crackle of lightning flashed across the sky. She wished Mum and Dad would come home. Electrical storms often came in summer and it could be dangerous to be out in them.

Chellie crept into bed, meaning to stay awake until her parents came in. But exhausted by all that had happened, she fell asleep.

She woke with the curtains flapping in her face like demented ghosts. The wind was screeching and shrieking like the violins of a class of learners. The pandanus outside her window was rattling like a cacophony of castanets. In the distance she could hear the drum roll of surf on Turtle Beach. She groped for the light switch. Nothing happened. She grabbed her torch and shouted. 'Mum! Dad!'

But there was no answer.

Where they still out in the storm?

Chellie raced into her parents' bedroom.

'Are you all right, Chellie?' they called.

Chellie jumed onto the bed and burrowed between them. 'I'm just so glad you're home,' she murmured.

'The hatchlings made it to the water before all this blew up,' Dad assured her.

Chellie snuggled close. Home Beach was more sheltered, and they would not have had to front the big rollers which would have dumped them, stunned them, perhaps even suffocated them. She sighed with relief and fell asleep. The rain, the lightning, the thunder became part of a bad dream.

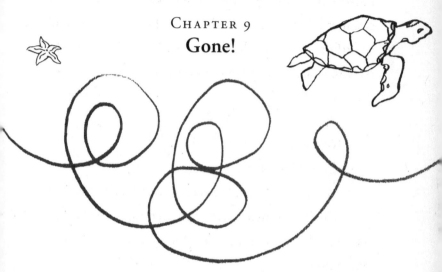

CHAPTER 9
Gone!

IN THE MORNING MUM SURVEYED the battered sweet corn, yesterday so tall and proud. Dad tinkered with the generator. Only the birds were singing. Chellie ran through the swishing wet bush to the rain-pocked sandhills. The sea was calming now, as if its roaring and giant waves had only been part of her dream. But it had been no dream. Clots of foam as big and white as enamel camping plates were bowling along the beach. And the sand was littered with clumps of brown seaweed, like the dung of a vast herd of mythical seacows.

But of Caretta there was no sign.

Chellie scrambled down and ran along the bank of sea wrack. Had the high tide dumped her here among the very refuse which had brought about her death? She searched from one end of the beach to the other and back again, in case she had missed the brown shell somewhere among the mounds of seaweed. But there was no sign of her.

Caretta was gone.

Chellie ran home. The generator was humming. Dad was helping Mum prop up the sweet corn and re-stake the tomatoes.

'Caretta's gone!'

Mum and Dad straightened up.

'The sea has claimed its own,' Dad said. 'She's where she belongs, Chellie.'

Chellie nodded. Her mouth felt too dry to speak, but her eyes felt wet.

'Let's all go down and search together,' Dad suggested. 'Three pairs of eyes are better than one.'

Chellie nodded again. It was true. Her eyes had been blurry while she searched.

Together they combed all that the sea had cast up overnight. But Caretta was nowhere to be found.

'She's gone back to where she belongs,' Dad repeated, trying to comfort Chellie.

But Chellie could only think of all those hungry mouths in the sea. She did not want to think of them swallowing Caretta's eggs, their teeth tearing at Caretta's flippers, her tail, her head. Tears rolled down her sun-warmed cheeks.

Dad seemed to know what she was imagining. 'It's the chain of life, Chellie. We're all part of it.'

Chellie nodded. She knew. But if only Caretta had laid her eggs. If only her babies would be hatching soon . . .

Chapter 10
The Campaign Begins

THAT VERY DAY CHELLIE BEGAN to attack the rubbish.

There was just so *much* of it.

But first of all she gathered a posy of seaweeds – brown, golden, pink, white, crimson, green – and took it down to the water's edge, letting it float away back to the depths where it had come from.

'Goodbye, Caretta,' she whispered. 'I'll never forget you.'

The tide which had taken Caretta always brought in all sorts of natural objects. Usually Chellie loved to discover seaweed in all its varieties, coconuts, mangrove pencils, hoop pine fronds, driftwood, shells, sponges, coral, feathers, even the occasional dead seabird or fish among the flotsam.

But now she was determined to deal with the jetsam, the human rubbish which also came in with the tide.

That afternoon Chellie filled five big garbage bags.

There were take-away food boxes, spoons, forks and plastic cups, cigarette lighters – and soggy cigarette butts. Yuk! Poisonous for turtles as well as people. Drink cans, ring pulls, corks and bottle stoppers with nasty sharp metal catches. Drinking straws galore. Sweets wrappers of shiny cellophane and foil, tempting to turtles. Toothbrushes too. At least some people on boats cleaned their teeth, Chellie thought.

They must have had parties on their pleasure craft, because Chellie found limp balloons, which looked deceptively like colourful reef fish, but were lethal to sea creatures. Ribbons from presents too, pretty on a parcel but terrible for turtles. There were broken sunglasses and goggles; an occasional cap or hat; and thongs, dozens and dozens of them. Different sizes and colours, some broken, some quite new. Sandals too. And shoes. Even fishermen's rubber boots. Enough footwear for a centipede.

Chellie decided to separate the trash into different sorts. A bag for footwear, another for take-away containers, and one for stuff like cans, wrappers, ribbon, rubber gloves and toothbrushes. The most dangerous things – rope, twine, netting, fishing line, rubber straps and those plastic binding strips – would need stronger bags. The ropes were so heavy they simply burst the garbage bags. The plastic bags and sheeting, all sand-caked, also needed a sturdier bag. So did the eels of black rubber hose and sections of polythene pipe.

Bottles were a major item. There were scores and scores of them. Lids too – a confetti of lids of all colours. And glass bottles. Chellie examined each glass bottle she found in case it contained a message. But none did. The message was the bottles themselves.

She lugged the bags up onto the sandbank. No use leaving them where the sea could reach them and release their deadly contents again. But this was just one afternoon's work. What *was* she going to *do* with all this stuff?

She'd have to discuss it with Dad. And this was only the beginning. Heaps of rubbish had accumulated over years, not only on Turtle Beach, but on all the other seven beaches too. Chellie remembered what Dad had said: one for each day of the week, and one over. She would have to organise a calendar. A beach a day. Every week. Because the sea was not going to stop spewing up the garbage. And people were not going to stop throwing rubbish off their boats.

Or were they?

Could she start a campaign to encourage boaties to be more careful, more caring, more aware of the harm they were causing, more aware of the turtles they were killing by dumping their junk overboard?

As she trudged home, Chellie wondered what she could do. Write some letters maybe to the fishermen's cooperatives, to the cruising yacht clubs?

Dad was sympathetic. 'You're right, Chellie. First we have to deal with the rubbish already on the island. We've got to corral it so it doesn't escape again. Let's build some pens – we can use that wire netting from the old chook yard. And the chook feed bags will be just the thing for collecting the heavy stuff. Garbage bags weren't designed for that.'

'I thought I could write some letters, too,' Chellie said.

Dad nodded. 'Good idea. We can find some addresses on the web. These organisations have news-letters. They might publish your emails.'

Chellie and Dad built a row of rubbish pens, each a metre high and a metre square, on a flat stretch of sandbank above Turtle Beach. Chellie pulled out some chicken pellet bags from the shed. She took down the calendar and wrote the name of a beach on each day of the week. Then she and Dad had a session on the computer, finding addresses to which Chellie could write.

'Go to it,' Dad urged. Chellie needed no urging. Her fingers began to fly over the keyboard.

Dear Fishing Boat Crews,
I live with my Mum and Dad on an island off the Queensland coast. Our island has eight beaches where turtles nest. This week, one of the mother turtles died because she was choked by fishing line. She was a loggerhead and loggerheads are an ENDANGERED species. The problem is that they feed on jellyfish, and often mistake fishing line and plastic bags and bottles for food. But of course these things KILL them.

So PLEASE PLEASE be careful not to throw such things off your boats into the sea. I've read that even whales die from swallowing plastic, and we don't want to lose any more whales, do we?

The sea doesn't want to be a garbage dump either, so it washes as much junk as it can onto the beaches. You ought to see the rubbish on our island. Since the beautiful loggerhead died, I have started to pick it up so that it doesn't get back into the water. Today I filled up five big garbage bags with rope and twine and netting and fishing line, and those horrible lures with barbs, and plastic, and plastic bags and bottles. Even POISON bottles!

But even after I've cleaned up the beach we still have a problem: what do we do with all the junk on our island? Our island isn't a garbage tip. We use all our kitchen scraps for compost in the garden, and buy our stores in recyclable containers. SO PLEASE PLEASE DON'T THROW YOUR STUFF INTO THE SEA.

PLEASE THINK OF THE TURTLES. The loggerheads are ENDANGERED and the green turtles are VULNERABLE. Turtles have been living in the sea for over 1 MILLION YEARS! But only seven species have survived. PLEASE don't let plastic and fishing gear be the death of them too.

(Signed) Chelonia Green (which means Green turtle)

PS. My real name is Michelle Braddon. Mum and Dad call me Chellie. I do school with Distance Education.

Dad and Mum read the letter.

'That's great!' Dad exclaimed.

Mum was pleased too. 'Shows you're a good student in the School of Distance Education.'

'You're such a good teacher, Mum.' Chellie hugged her. 'I can use the same letter for the boaties, can't I? I'll put in about the balloons and the ribbon to them too.'

'Go for it,' Dad said. 'And I hope they publish them in their newsletters.'

Chapter 11
So Much to Do

Next day Chellie went back to see the turtles. She wanted to, and yet she didn't want to. She didn't want to see Caretta's little pool empty. But she didn't want to see it occupied by another turtle either.

It wasn't.

It was empty empty empty. Chellie turned away and went to sit near her green family. There weren't so many turtles today. Perhaps some of the females had finished their egg-laying and had set off back to their feeding grounds. Chellie sat dreaming of them on their long journey, dreaming of the tropical coasts they would reach. Occasionally one of the somnolent chelonia would raise its head and look at her. Even though she was careful never to let her shadow fall on the pool, the turtles always knew she was there. Just one of the family come to visit. Chellie was comforted by their quiet acceptance.

When she went back to continue the clean-up, Dad and Mum were already at work – Dad at one end of the beach, Mum at the other.

'Many hands make light work,' Mum smiled. 'We won't be able to help you every day, but we will when we can.'

Chellie set to. So much to do. Turtle Beach was the biggest and the worst for flotsam and jetsam. But then there were Oystercatcher Cove, Snowy Beach, Curlew Beach, Orchid Beach, South Beach and Pine Cove. A long way to lug rubbish back from them. Home Beach still had to be done too. Today, Chellie decided, she would concentrate on rope and twine, fishing net and lines. She wondered how far they would stretch if she laid all the pieces end on end. A hundred metres she was sure. Two hundred metres more likely.

Angrily she tugged at heavy, thick ropes half

buried in the sand. A big storm could uncover them and set them free. She yanked at piece after piece after piece of twine – orange, blue, green, yellow – entangled in swirls of seaweed. She pulled at netting snagged on driftwood and pounced on every tangle of fishing line that gleamed like onion skin oh so innocently among coconuts and knobby, pineapple-like pandanus fruits.

At last Mum called, 'That's enough for today. You can come back tomorrow and every day until school starts. I'm going home now. Why don't you go and tell Dad to knock off? I'll have scones made by the time you get home.'

Normally Chellie would have skipped or run or taken flying leaps along to the far end where Dad was. But today she just walked. Slowly, soberly.

At the end of the beach, before the rocks began and the cliffs reared up, waves and wind had created an extra big sandbank. And lots of junk somehow got swept into this corner.

Dad beckoned. 'Come and look at this.'

What had he found? Chellie's footsteps quickened. Could it be Caretta? She ran the last fifty metres.

But it wasn't Caretta. Dad was pointing to the sandbank. Jetsam was embedded at intervals all the way up – a broken piece of propeller; the yellow plastic lid of an ice-cream container; a red thong; the sleeve of a checked shirt; the staring, blue-eyed head of one of those horrible lures; and a score of other things.

'It'll be an archaeologist's dig in a hundred years' time,' Dad exclaimed. 'Some researcher will be thrilled to find all these traces of the way we lived. Like Pompeii or some of those sites in the Middle East.'

Chellie loved Dad's enthusiasm for seeing possibilities. But she didn't know whether to be pleased or sorry that it was not Caretta. Caretta, mangled, decomposing, only recognisable by her shell. Perhaps one day the sea would bring back her beautiful shell.

CHAPTER 12

Hope by Helicopter

DAY AFTER DAY THROUGH THREE hot January weeks Chellie toiled, filling bag after bag so that Dad had to build more bins. She managed to clean up Oystercatcher Cove, and Mum and Dad helped with Home Beach. But she was feeling discouraged. So much rubbish. Just so much. Nothing but rubbish every day. Battens, planks, a hatch cover, a ripped sail, even flower pots. And the never-ending bottles and plastic. Chellie began to think that all the world's garbage was being tipped into the sea every day, and that an awful lot was ending up on their island.

Eagerly, anxiously she checked the email, hoping that someone would write back. A note arrived from the turtle research people thanking her for the information about Caretta. But the fishermen and cruising yacht clubs did not acknowledge her plea, let alone say they would publish it. Nothing came from them at all.

Before it was time to turn the page on the new calendar, the school term started.

'Tell me about what you did in the holidays,' Chellie's teacher asked. She always wanted to know that. So Chellie emailed her story about Caretta and her letter to the fishermen and boaties. She also wrote an update about all the garbage she had collected and how much remained to be cleared. Then she settled down to tackle her first worksheets. But before she had finished, the phone rang. Her mother answered it.

'It's for you, Michelle.'

It was her teacher.

'That's a sad story, Michelle,' Miss Howe said, 'but you've written it beautifully. And you showed a lot of initiative in sending those letters and starting the clean-up. I'm really proud of you. I have a friend who is the environmental writer for a national newspaper. Do you mind if I show it to him?'

Chellie gasped. 'Wow! You mean my story might be in the paper?'

'Well . . . I can't promise that. But he might be able to write something about it.'

'Hooray! That would reach lots more fishermen and boaties and people who litter. More than *I* could ever do,' Chellie babbled. 'Oh, yes! Please show it to him. Maybe he could come and see for himself.'

'Perhaps,' said Miss Howe. 'Don't get your hopes up. It's not easy to get an article in the paper. But I'm sure he'll be interested in what you've written and what you're doing.'

Chellie hugged Mum. 'She likes my story. She's going to show it to a journalist!'

She rushed off to tell Dad too.

'Why don't you do what you talked about earlier?' Dad suggested. 'Measure all the rope and stuff from Turtle Beach. Collect some statistics. You can do it for a maths assignment. I'll help.'

So Chellie and Dad set off for Turtle Beach with his reel of measuring tape.

'We should have done this when we started,'

Chellie panted as they emptied two bins of rope and netting and heaved it back down onto the beach. 'Maybe after we've measured this lot I could do it day by day. Keep a tally.'

'Good idea,' Dad grunted. 'This is hard work.'

Dragging and pulling, they gradually laid it out end to end above the high tide mark. At last it was finished, a great long stretch of rope, twine, netting and fishing line snaking along the beach like a huge boa constrictor.

'How long is it, Dad?'

'I reckon nearly two hundred metres.'

'We'll just have to estimate the length of the knotted bits and tangles,' Chellie puffed.

Carefully they measured it with the tape. Chellie whooped when they passed the one-hundred-metre mark, and whooped even louder when the tape reached its full length a second time.

'Two hundred plus,' Dad announced, pacing it out to the end. 'Two hundred and thirty-one metres, and then some for the tangles.'

'Let's leave it here to show Mum tomorrow,' Chellie suggested.

Dad nodded. 'Okay. The sea won't be up this high

overnight as it's a neap tide and there's no sign of wind. Should be all right.'

In the morning Mum insisted that Chellie do her lessons before they went to Turtle Beach. Chellie was longing to be off, but she had settled down to complete her worksheets when she heard the throbbing of an aircraft.

'It's a helicopter,' she shouted, throwing down her pen and rushing outside. Light planes often went over, but a helicopter was rare. Perhaps it was Customs officers, or a search and rescue.

The whirring grew louder and louder as the helicopter came into view. Chellie waved excitedly as it hovered over the house but sighed as it moved away. Then she shouted, 'It's going to land on Turtle Beach!'

Lessons were forgotten as all the family followed the chopper, watching it drop below the hill, then hearing the silence after its motor stopped.

Who could it be?

Chellie was speechless with excitement and exertion. She was running at record speed.

Could it really be Miss Howe's friend, the journalist? Would he really write about Caretta and the rubbish?

As they topped the sandhills they could see the helicopter squatting in the middle of the beach like a giant dragonfly. Three men were climbing out. Three.

Who were they? A pilot. And who were the others?

Chellie took a running jump down the bank and sprinted across to the strangers. They were smiling.

'You must be Chelonia Green,' the tallest said. 'Your teacher, Miss Howe, showed me your story and told me what you are doing to try to protect the turtles. I'd like to write an article for my paper about it.'

Chellie nodded, too excited to speak.

'I'm Mark and this is Peter who will take some photos, if that's OK with your parents. And this is Bill, our pilot.'

Dad and Mum were just approaching. Mark introduced his companions and asked again about permission to take photos and do a story about Chellie and the turtles and her campaign against litter. Dad and Mum beamed.

'If it makes people think and helps cut down pollution of the sea even a little,' Dad said, 'it will be well worthwhile.'

'And saves some turtles,' Chellie added, recovering

her voice. 'Maybe some whales. And dugongs too. They're all affected. Come and see what we've collected in just over three weeks.'

Mark smiled at her and followed. He made notes about the rope boa constrictor and all the bins of bottles and thongs and plastic and assorted refuse, while the photographer got to work.

'It's pretty impressive, what you've done, Chelonia Green,' Mark said. 'There should be more people like you.'

'More people not throwing rubbish overboard would be better,' Chellie replied. 'I don't want to pick up other people's rubbish all my life. I want to go to university and become a marine biologist. Now, do you want to see the turtles? The tide's right if we don't dawdle.' She led the way to the turtle pool and introduced her family one by one.

The three visitors were entranced. 'I've never seen anything like this!' Mark exclaimed softly. The others nodded in silent agreement.

Chellie smiled at her new friends. 'I come here most days to watch them, when the tide's right. But I haven't been able to come so often since I started collecting the litter.'

'Your chopper will be safe here on the beach,' Dad said to Bill. 'Why don't you all come back to the house and have a cuppa before you leave. We keep records and photos you might like to see.'

The pilot looked at his watch. 'I've got another job after this, but we can spare an hour.'

Chellie had never known an hour to go so quickly. She and Mum and Dad all went back to Turtle Beach to watch the helicopter take off. Bill checked his watch again, then looked at Chellie. 'There's just time to give you a buzz over the island. Hop in!'

Chellie didn't need to be asked twice.

Peter strapped her in. 'I need the door open so I can take photos.'

Chellie waved to Mum and Dad as the chopper lifted and steadied. 'Don't go over the turtle pool, the noise might disturb them' she shouted to the pilot above the roar.

So they headed away overland. Chellie looked down on the house and the vegetable garden. The chooks, alarmed by the strange noise, scattered into the long grass. She looked down on the gullies where the fruit bats roosted, and down on the clifftops and the red earth gulches. Her island. Her home.

Within minutes they were back on the beach and she was scrambling out.

'Thank you, thank you!' she shouted as the helicopter lifted again.

As it chuttered away into the distance, Chellie blinked. Had it really happened?

'Come on, Chellie,' Dad said. 'We'd better make sure the boa constrictor doesn't escape on tonight's tide.'

With Mum helping it did not take as long to gather the rope up again as it had to lay it out, so there was still time to do some more collecting. Chellie picked up the empty bags and went off with new heart. If only Mark's article made it into the paper . . .

CHAPTER 13

Tracks!

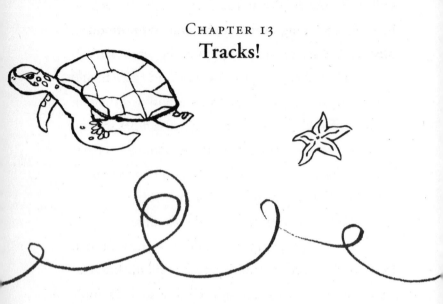

OVER THE NEXT TWO DAYS Chellie collected on South Beach and Pine Cove. Then on Friday she made her way to Snowy Beach. It was quite a trudge: across to Turtle Beach, over the point to Oystercatcher Cove, and then around the rocks. A pair of ospreys circled over the clifftops watching her, and two fishing boats were moving north on the horizon.

'Don't you dare drop any of your rubbish,' Chellie muttered, scowling at them. 'I'm just sick of clearing up after careless people.'

After a last hop, jump and scramble, Chellie smiled as Snowy Beach came into sight. It was so beautiful, gleaming in the bright sunlight, untrodden, pristine. Except for the rubbish. Chellie set to work. It was a long beach, almost as long as Turtle Beach, and she had decided to do it in sections. Ignoring the jetsam already accumulating again in the three sections she had done, she strode on towards the distant end of the glittering expanse. Bending down to scoop up a twist of lethal green twine, she suddenly stopped.

What were those tracks in the sand?

Above the high-tide mark. Pitted by rain. Blurred by wind. But tracks. Definitely tracks. Old turtle tracks, which had survived the storm. Chellie knelt carefully beside them. Green turtle tracks show distinctive front-flipper marks. But these were distinctive hind-flipper marks. The loggerhead pattern. Yes! They were loggerhead tracks. Caretta's? Yes! They had to be Caretta's. She must have laid her eggs after all.

Chellie jumped up and ran. Up the snowy sandhills, plunging down through the gully, over stony outcrops, through the grass which swayed around her shoulders, hurdling scratchy bushes. Yelling at the top of her voice. 'Out of the way, snakes! Out of the way!'

'Dad! Mum!' she yelled, long before they could hear her. But Dad looked up from the pump he was fixing and saw her pelting down the hill. He called and Mum came out of the house.

Chellie panted up to them, red-faced, sweating, half laughing, half crying. 'I've found Caretta's tracks on Snowy Beach. She must have laid her eggs there. Come and see!'

'That's wonderful,' her parents exclaimed together, almost as excited as she was.

'But cool off for a moment and have a drink before we go,' Mum urged.

And Dad said, 'Yes, do. They won't go away.'

Chellie was bursting with impatience, but she gulped down the water that Mum gave her, grabbed three oranges and tugged at her parents. 'Come on. Hurry up.'

Going back the way she had come, she described her find. 'They're loggerhead tracks, Dad. Remember how you showed me those photos. They're different from the green. They must be Caretta's. They must be.'

'Could be,' Dad concurred. 'She's the only loggerhead we know of around here. She could have laid a clutch before she died.'

'They are hers,' Chellie declared firmly. 'I just know they are. And the eggs will be hatching soon. Any night now.'

'You're right,' Dad agreed. 'Probably this weekend.'

They pushed up through the thick green bush of the gully onto the sandhill beyond. They always approached Snowy Beach from the shore, so the sight of it stretching out below took Chellie by surprise. They paused for a moment looking down on the scene of brilliant white and vivid blue.

'Spectacular!' Dad exclaimed.

'Heavenly,' Mum added.

Chellie smiled, inside and out. Caretta's Beach.

Following her own footprints she led the way down to the tracks. 'There!' she pointed triumphantly.

Dad and Mum knelt down beside them.

'You're right, Chellie,' Dad beamed. 'It's a loggerhead's track. Well spotted.'

Mum hugged her.

'If she laid those eggs at December full moon, they should be hatching soon,' Dad calculated.

'Let's camp out and watch,' Chellie urged.

'It's not a good forecast for camping out tonight,' Mum demurred. 'Looks like rain. But maybe tomorrow.'

'Please, oh please,' Chellie begged. She began collecting rubbish as if her life, as well as the turtles', depended on it.

Mum and Dad helped for a while. Then Dad said, 'We need to make some bins here too. I'll go home and see what wire I can find.'

After her parents left, Chellie sat beside Caretta's tracks, willing the baby turtles not to emerge until she could be there. She wondered too about Mark's article. They hadn't heard anything from him. Would it get into the paper? And if so, when? Shadows from the sandhills started creeping down the beach and the sea began to glow as the sky faded to lavender and gold. Chellie suddenly realised how hungry she was and set off home. Not around the rocks. Not at dusk. Back over the sandhills and ploughing through the bush.

Mum was looking out for her, waving and calling. Chellie began to run. What had happened?

'Miss Howe phoned to tell you that Mark's article and photos will be published tomorrow! In a special Australia Day supplement about the environment!'

Chellie grabbed Mum and began to dance. It was even better than she had hoped.

She ran to tell Dad who was dragging wire netting out from bushes behind the old chook yard.

'Well done, Chellie! Thousands of people will read that!'

Mum made pancakes for tea to celebrate. Chellie loved pancakes and ate until she was as full as one of her garbage bags. She was so excited she thought she would never be able to sleep. But the soothing sound of Mum's rain lulled her into another world.

Chellie woke to the chug of a boat engine. And voices across the water. She jumped out of bed and ran to look. It was a sparkling, rain-freshened morning. A white yacht and a blue fishing boat were anchored out near the home buoy. A yellow inflatable – a rubber duckie – full of people was putt-putting towards the beach, and other people were casting off in a dinghy from the fishing boat.

Who were they?

Chapter 14
Help Arrives

Chellie gulped some milk, gobbled a banana and ran down to the beach. There were three kids as well as two adults in the rubber duckie. What fun! Chellie didn't often have other kids to play with. But they hadn't come to play. As they waded ashore, Chellie could see that they were carrying garbage bags.

'Hi! You must be Chelonia Green!' the big boy greeted her. 'I'm Tim.' He was the oldest and obviously the leader, Chellie decided.

'I thought your letter was cool,' the girl said. She was about Chellie's age. 'I'm Jacinta.'

She'll do, Chellie murmured to herself.

'And I'm Will,' the small boy piped up. 'We've come to help.'

'That's great! Did you see the article in the paper?' Chellie asked.

'No. What article?' her three new friends chorused.

Their tall, cheerful father, anchor in left hand, stretched out his right. 'I owe you an apology, Chelonia. I'm John, editor of the cruising yacht club magazine you sent an email to. I'm sorry I didn't acknowledge it. We were away. But it's going into our next newsletter and our family certainly want to help. OK if we moor for the day and come ashore?'

The children's mother, with a picnic basket over her arm, put out her hand. ' I'm Sally,' she smiled. 'We'd love to meet your parents.'

Chellie could only grin.

Mum and Dad came down the beach as the dinghy from the fishing boat, with two kids and two adults aboard, nosed in. A stocky, weather-beaten man hopped out nimbly.

'I'm Ted from the fishermen's co-op. Sorry I didn't have time to answer your email, Chelonia Green, but our family is here now to help you clean up some of my fellow fishermen's junk. Careless coots, my lot. But I'm putting your message on our website, so hopefully they might be a bit more careful and there mightn't be so much rubbish in future. This is my wife, Joan, and the kids, Jack and Alice.'

Jack, probably a year younger than Tim, had broad shoulders and a smile almost as wide. Sweet-faced little Alice, plump and rosy like her mother, made Chellie think of a peach.

Chellie was lost for words. But she managed to ask, 'Did you see the article in today's paper?'

Ted laughed. 'Today's paper wasn't even printed when we left port yesterday. A pity they have to use white paper now for fish and chips, or more people might read it.'

Chellie grinned even wider. She liked Ted. This was going to be a fun day. Like a party. A birthday party for Caretta's babies, maybe.

'Would you like to see the turtles before we start on the rubbish collecting?' Chellie asked everyone.

'Yes, please,' was the emphatic answer.

So, taking picnic baskets, off they went.

Turtle Beach was looking its loveliest: wide and shining, scalloped with lacy foam as the sea receded.

'We have to be quiet. We don't want to disturb the turtles,' Chellie warned. 'And there may not be many, as some have probably laid all their six clutches by now and gone back to sea.'

She led the visitors carefully across the rocks of Turtle Point. When they gazed down into the big pool, the looks on their faces thrilled her. Nine more instant turtle lovers.

Jacinta thought she could have gazed at the turtles all day, but Chellie announced, 'Time to go to work.'

Except that it was more like fun than work, because Chellie organised it like a treasure hunt.

'The men can do the ropes and twine and fishing stuff, because they're heavy. Tim, Will and Jack can collect the big plastic, and Jacinta, Alice and I will do bottles and small plastics. The Mums can do thongs and house things. Let's do the whole beach like it's never been done before and meet back here at the bins for lunch.'

The men inspected the bins, already full almost to overflowing.

'Looks as if there's another job for us, Ted,' John remarked, 'moving this stuff back to an onshore dump.'

Dad beamed. 'That would be really helpful. I'm running out of chicken wire to make more bins.'

'Consider it done,' Ted declared. 'Back to the mainland where it came from.'

Everyone spread out along the beach, picking, pulling, dragging, tugging, exclaiming over what they found. Chellie had never seen so many people on any of their beaches, never seen so much activity. When they met up again, bags were bulging and the visitors were shocked by the amount of rubbish.

'You should have seen it before Chellie started her blitz,' Dad told them.

'It was the beach of a billion bottles!' Mum added. 'But many hands make light work.'

'The beach hasn't been this clean since before Captain Cook and Matthew Flinders sailed along this coast,' Chellie beamed. Who's for a swim?'

Everyone raced down to the water, chasing and splashing each other, squealing and laughing. It was the best fun Chellie had ever had.

After lunch, it didn't take long to clean up the latest flotsam and jetsam in Oystercatcher Cove before moving to Snowy Beach. Chellie was pleased that no one complained about the rock hopping and scrambling, not even Alice who had the shortest legs. Will, who was not much bigger, was as surefooted as Chellie herself.

'I haven't done as much work here as on Turtle Beach,' she explained. 'So there's lots to clear up. But there's a special spot I'll show you where we don't want to compact the sand.' Chellie led the way to the loggerhead tracks, telling the story of Caretta as they walked.

'You mean those eggs might be hatching any minute?' Tim asked.

'Those baby turtles might come out tonight?' squeaked Will.

'Oh please, can we stay and watch?' Jacinta pleaded with her parents.

Jack and Alice joined the chorus.

'We've never seen baby turtles on their way to the sea.'

'And we've got our sleeping bags.'

The parents all looked at each other. Chellie held her breath.

'We'll have to douse the campfire early,' Dad decreed. 'It might confuse the hatchlings.' So it was settled. Chellie flashed a smile at Dad.

While Dad and the mothers went back for sleeping bags and food, lots of it, the cleaning gang got busy, scouring every square metre of sea wrack halfway along the beach.

The sky was turning watermelon pink when Dad and the mothers returned, laden like packhorses with camping gear and enough food for twelve hungry people.

'Let's get the cooking done before dark,' Dad said, building a fire round a big billy containing saveloys, and banking it up with heavier wood to make coals for damper and grilling chops.

Chellie loved to watch the green and blue flames spurting and flaring from the driftwood. So, it seemed, did the others. Everyone stood around, listening to the hiss of the fire and the lap of the waves.

'I'll never forget this,' Jacinta whispered to Chellie, and Alice squeezed her hand.

The first stars were beginning to show like moth holes

in a dark blue blanket when Dad doused the fire and scuffed a thick layer of sand over the coals. Then he explained how they had to wait and watch in stillness and silence away from the nest area.

'I'll have a special torch to check on developments, if any, from time to time. But it's a waiting game, and you have to remember this mightn't be the night anyway. So don't be disappointed if nothing happens.'

The dry sand where they squatted was still blood warm, the beach beyond was silver cool and the sea was blue as midnight. It seemed to Chellie as if they were in a magic circle, mesmerised by the crooning of the waves and the first call of the curlews.

In her mind's eye she could see Caretta emerging from the water, making her way up the beach where she had been born. She watched her laboriously digging her body pit, excavating her egg chamber. She could see the eggs dropping one by one, silvery, like Christmas baubles in the moonlight, could see Caretta covering them over, backfilling the big pit, setting off back to the sea. Hungry probably after all that effort. Seizing a morsel that glinted temptingly in the moonlit water. Choking. Entangled in the wicked fishing line. Choking choking choking. Starving, starving slowly. To death.

Chellie shivered and Jacinta moved closer on one side and Alice on the other. Chellie was grateful for their warmth, their friendship, their care. She wanted to see Caretta's babies emerge, but somehow now she wanted it even more for these others who had come to help.

A star fell. A small bat flittered by. A lone oystercatcher shrilled its peeping cry. Then suddenly the sand stirred in the centre of the magic circle. Slightly. Or had it? Eyes strained to confirm what they had seen. Yes, there it was again. A ripple. Just a slight ripple. Dad shone his shaded torch. Yes! There was a wee dark head appearing from the sand. And another. And another. Suddenly the sand was erupting with turtles. Tiny little creatures with shells no longer than Chellie's little finger, smaller even than green turtle hatchlings. Caretta's babies. The protective circle parted to let them pass.

Everyone held their breath as the turtles headed towards the sea. Scurrying, hurrying towards their new life. Chellie tried to count and thought she reached one hundred and seventeen. One hundred and seventeen little loggerheads.

'Go, little turtles, go! Stay safe, stay strong, grow, grow, grow. And come back again. Please do.'

Quietly, at a respectful distance, they followed the hatchlings down to the water. Watched them slip into their new home – swimming easily, naturally, gracefully, young as they were.

As the last turtle disappeared into a gentle wavelet everyone let out a sigh of relief – a deep breath of exhilaration – and turned in silence to hug each other. Together they had watched this special miracle.

Chellie was smiling, but the tears were running down her cheeks. Caretta's babies. The odds were against them, she knew. *But please, please, let one of them survive. Let at least one come back. Thirty years on. Even if I'm not here to see it.*

They walked to where the sleeping bags were already laid out. Still nobody spoke. The moment was too deep for words. They gathered in a circle again around the nest, and although she could barely see, Chellie knew that everyone was smiling. It was a night they would never forget.

Chapter 15
'Best Two Days of My Life'

When Chellie woke – Jacinta on one side and Alice on the other – everyone was stirring, crawling out of sleeping bags, stretching. So it wasn't a dream, she thought as she rubbed the sleep out of her eyes.

'Swim before breakfast?' Dad shouted, and everyone raced down the beach, laughing and joking. The kids were having so much fun that it was only the smell of bacon that finally lured them out of the water. After the bacon and eggs were eaten and the billy boiled, they made toast on the coals and spread it thick with

Mum's chunky lime marmalade.

'That's the best breakfast I've ever had,' Tim declared. And everyone agreed.

They shook the sand out of their sleeping bags, rolled them up and tidied the campsite.

'Now, what are the orders for the day, Captain Chellie?' Ted enquired.

'More of the same,' Chellie announced. 'We've still got the rest of this beach to do.'

So off they went with bags and crates to make Snowy Beach as clean as its name.

At lunchtime John and Ted conferred.

'We thought we'd bring the boats round here and to Turtle Beach to load. Anyone want a trip on a smelly fishing boat?' Ted enquired.

'Yes please!' Tim's, Jacinta's and Will's hands shot up.

'Could we come with you, John?' Jack and Alice asked. 'We've never been on a yacht.'

Chellie was torn. She had never been on a yacht *or* a fishing boat. Dad had a catamaran and a barge. His workhorses, he called them. 'Could I come round on one and back on the other?' she asked.

'Why not?' said Ted cheerfully. 'I can take all the camping gear from here too. Save humping it overland.'

They went back around the rocks, where Tim and Jack prised out some big lengths of rope that Chellie had never been able to budge, and sharp-eyed Will found fishing line in rock pools which had been underwater yesterday. Turtle Beach stretched smooth and hard and empty.

'Perfect for cricket,' Tim commented.

'Good idea,' Dad replied. 'But we don't have a ball.'

'I found a ball yesterday,' Will piped up. He pulled it out of his pocket. 'Look, it still bounces!'

'And I can make a bat.' Jack seized a small piece of plank and yanked a discarded fishing glove over one end for a grip.

'Game on,' Tim declared. 'Your first bowl, Chellie. And you bat first, Jack.'

It was a hilarious game. Chellie bowled, chased the ball, swung the bat, and laughed and laughed. Playing with just Mum and Dad was never so much fun.

All too soon it was time to stop and move on. At Home Beach they clambered into the dinghy and duckie and headed for the boats. Chellie climbed aboard *Sweet Alice*.

'I wish I had a boat named after me,' she exclaimed.

'It's a bit of a tradition among fishermen to name your boat after your mother or wife or daughter,' Ted explained. 'My mother was Alice, too.'

Chellie loved seeing the island from the water. It looked so dramatic with its cliffs and coves and rocky headlands. She pointed out some of her favourite places. They chugged past Turtle Beach, Turtle Point, Oyster-catcher Cove and the long rocky stretch where the ospreys were circling on updrafts.

'Wouldn't it be great to be able to fly like that!' Tim marvelled.

Chellie wondered if he wanted to be a pilot.

Dad had come too, to guide the fishing boat safely in to Snowy Beach.

'There's a patch of rocks that's sometimes uncovered,' he warned Ted. They anchored as close as possible to shore to make the loading easier. All the Snowy Beach rubbish had been left in bags and crates.

'We can stow the crates in the well.' Ted knew all about getting as much as possible aboard *Sweet Alice*.

At last the work was finished and they headed back to Turtle Beach to lend a hand.

Emptying the bins onto tarps and dragging them down the beach, into the dinghy and aboard the lovely yacht was quite a challenge. Chellie felt sad to see all the ugly debris piled on the decks. But John was not worried. He saw it as a photo opportunity. Whipping out a camera he took several shots.

'I'll publish these on the club website. Should make crews a bit more careful.' He hopped into the duckie and paddled across to take some snaps aboard *Sweet Alice* too.

Ted was pleased. 'A picture's worth a thousand words, they say.' Looking at Chellie he hastened to add, 'But if it hadn't been for your words in the first place, there'd be no pictures. We would never have come to the island.'

The yacht had puttered round using her engine, but John had hoisted the sails for Chellie's benefit.

'*Wind Chime* is a perfect name for her,' Chellie sighed to Jacinta, who with Tim and Will had swapped back to their own boat. 'She's so beautiful.'

She seemed to glide like a gull over the glassy green waters. As they rounded the southern end of the island, the westering sun turned the sea to gold, and the sound of the wind in the rigging and sails changed from a whisper to a song.

They had a barbecue on Home Beach, watching the sun slide into the sea and the clouds turn into full-blown roses: pink and gold and apricot. Mum brought out the visitors' book. There weren't many names in it, but the visitors from *Sweet Alice* and *Wind Chime* filled two pages with their enthusiastic comments. Chellie especially liked Jack's: 'Best two days of my life.'

'Watch our websites, Chellie. I'm sorry we didn't get round to all the beaches. But if we may,' John said to Chellie and her parents, 'we'd like to come again at Easter to help.'

'So would we,' Ted said, and all the kids shouted 'Yay!'

Chellie grinned.

'I'm hoping we'll be able to persuade other yachties to adopt an island, one of the uninhabited ones, and clean up the beaches once a year. I think the idea could catch on,' John added.

'A great idea,' Mum and Dad agreed.

'I could try the same with my lot,' Ted offered. 'Fishermen know the coast as well as anyone. It'll be a wake-up call for them to see the rubbish.'

So the Adopt an Island scheme was hatched, and Chellie knew she wouldn't be alone in her task any more. 'Could you publish a photo of Caretta too?' she asked. 'If people could see what one piece of fishing line did . . .'

'Sure will,' John and Ted promised. 'Just email it to us.'

Chellie hated saying goodbye to all her new friends. She and Dad and Mum stood at the water's edge watching the dinghy and the duckie head off to *Sweet Alice* and *Wind Chime*, and the lights twinkle after the families had gone aboard. They were leaving early next morning for their trips home. Chellie felt empty and full at the same time. Sad and happy.

Mum guessed how she felt. 'Not long till Easter,' she said. 'It's early this year.'

Chellie woke several times in the night and looked out to see two lights in Home Bay, and imagined Tim, Jacinta, Will, Jack and Alice snug in their bunks.

But in the morning when she woke, Home Bay was empty again.

CHAPTER 16
More Help

WHEN CHELLIE PULLED OUT HER worksheets and settled at the kitchen table, Mum said, 'You don't have to do lessons today. It's a holiday. Australia Day!' But Chellie felt so flat after all the excitement of the last two days she decided she might as well do them anyway. There was nothing else special, even if it was a holiday. Only more rubbish.

She was plugging away when she heard the distant drone of an aircraft. Surely it wasn't heading for the island? Not two aircraft in a week?

Out in the garden Mum heard it also. 'Chellie, come and look!'

Chellie rushed out. A little seaplane was flying towards Home Beach. She could see the floats quite clearly. A helicopter on Tuesday, a seaplane on Monday!

Dad came out of the shed and together they watched in amazement as the floatplane splashed down on the water, coming to rest like a big moth.

Who could it be this time?

They rushed down to the beach, dragging the canoes to the water's edge. Dad and Chellie jumped in and began paddling out to the plane. As they approached, the door opened and standing there smiling and waving was Chellie's teacher, Miss Howe!

'Miss Howe!' Chellie shouted. 'What are you doing here?' She manoeuvred her canoe alongside.

Miss Howe was holding up a newspaper. 'I thought you'd want to see this.'

Chellie whooped and almost overturned in excitement.

'Hold on,' Miss Howe said. 'Can I come ashore with you? I've brought some friends. We'd like to help your clean-up.' Chellie nodded, too overwhelmed to speak. Her teacher, in bright pink shorts and top, slid her long brown legs down and landed lightly behind her.

Now the pilot poked his head out. 'If you can take my three passengers ashore, I could take you and your parents up for a bit of a flip before we get down to business.'

Chellie goggled. A helicopter, a fishing boat, a yacht. And now a ride in a floatplane! 'Let's start now,' she agreed eagerly.

Dad picked up another woman from the plane and they paddled to shore in tandem.

'Come on, Mum,' Chellie urged. 'We're going for a trip in the plane!' Then she remembered her manners. 'Miss Howe has brought friends to help with the clean-up. And she's brought the paper!'

Mum climbed into Dad's canoe and they paddled back to the plane. Chellie and Mum clambered aboard and Dad ferried the last passenger, a man, ashore, then came back.

'OK,' said the pilot. 'I'm Jim. Strap yourselves in. We'll do a circuit of the island.' He revved up the engine, and the little plane skimmed across the bay and lifted.

Jim flew low, hugging the coastline. Chellie was almost dizzy with delight, looking down on the bays and beaches and bluffs. It was nearly as good as being an osprey. What a pity Tim couldn't be doing it. All too soon they were back at Home Bay.

On the kitchen table, where Chellie's worksheets still lay, Miss Howe had spread out the newspaper. Chellie gasped when she saw the cover of the supplement. The photo Dad had taken of her kneeling beside Caretta sat under the headline, CHELONIA GREEN – CHAMPION OF TURTLES. She read the story Mark had written about Caretta and the rubbish, and turned the page to find more photos – of the rope boa constrictor, of the bins of bottles and thongs and plastic, and of the turtles. Plus a big plea to everyone not to throw refuse into the sea.

It couldn't have been better.

'Thank you, Miss Howe. Thank you so much. This is great!' Chellie's face was glowing. 'Oh, I must write to thank Mark. Surely this will make a difference.'

To save time and a lot of rock-hopping and scrambling, Dad took everyone round to Curlew Beach in the catamaran. Chellie hoped the curlews wouldn't be disturbed by such an invasion, but it was too good a chance to miss for a complete clean sweep. They might even be able to do Orchid Beach as well, and still have time for a swim. She was glad Miss Howe had thought to bring a supply of heavy duty garbage bags, because quite a lot of the chicken pellet bags had been sent off holding yesterday's rubbish.

'It's a marathon job you've undertaken, Chellie,' Miss Howe said. 'Congratulations on sticking at it. Most people would have become discouraged and given up.'

Chellie had to admit she'd felt like that often. 'But if we save one turtle it's worth it.'

'You'll probably save more than that, as people get the message,' Miss Howe assured her. 'Of course, you'll never know. But you've done your best, and inspired other people to do their bit also. So that counts for a lot.'

They swam and snorkelled before lunch, and afterwards Chellie showed the visitors some curlew tracks and two curlews: silent, still, like shadows on the sand, standing in the shade of a casuarina. They cleaned up Orchid Beach too. Chellie was thrilled. She picked a spray of orchids for Miss Howe and gave her a little driftwood dragon for her desk.

'Have you time to see the turtles before you go?'

'We'd love to,' the helpers all exclaimed.

'We could take the plane to Turtle Beach,' Jim suggested. Chellie boggled at the thought. They loaded the rubbish into the catamaran and returned to Home Bay.

'Can we squeeze Chellie in?' Miss Howe asked Jim.

Chellie had worked out that Jim was Miss Howe's boyfriend. Surely he couldn't refuse? She held her breath and tried to look small as he glanced at her.

'Yep,' he grinned, 'if we don't take the rubbish. We can collect that when we drop her back.' Chellie climbed into the floatplane for the second time. It was too good to be true.

At Turtle Beach they waded from the plane along to Turtle Point. Chellie loved showing her special family to people who appreciated how remarkable and precious and how very vulnerable they were. The Chelonia Greens are getting quite a fan club, she giggled to herself.

'You'll have to write another instalment of your story now, Chellie,' Miss Howe observed as they said goodbye.

Chellie grinned. 'I'm going to do just that.'

CHAPTER 17
'Chelonia , You're a Champion!'

OVER THE NEXT WEEK THE days returned to normal. Lessons in the morning, a visit to the turtles, and rubbish collecting on one beach after another. The sea was throwing up just as much as ever and Chellie had to remind herself that it would continue that way for a while. Many boaties had been out cruising and partying over the Australia Day weekend and most of them probably had not got the message yet. Nor had the fishing crews. She just had to keep at it.

Think of Caretta's babies, she told herself. 'Sharks stay away, today and every day, from the baby turtles out in the bay. Noddies and boobies stay away, today and every day, from the baby turtles out in the bay. Hungry fish stay away, today and every day, from the baby turtles out in the bay.' Remember the good times with Mark and John's and Ted's families and Miss Howe and Jim and their friends.

The bags and bins started to fill again, but more hatchings at night along Home Beach encouraged her to persist. 'Go, little turtles, go! Stay safe, stay strong, grow, grow, grow. And come back again. Please do,' she chanted as she made and measured a new rope boa constrictor on each beach.

Statistics were important, Dad had said. So Chellie carried a notebook now and jotted down the tallies for each day. After all, if she was going to be a scientist and do research she had to have data. How much deadly rope, lines and fishing gear? How many plastic bags? How many plastic bottles? How many thongs and all those miscellaneous items? Dad had suggested the miscellaneous category. It covered a lot of stuff.

Emails came from Tim, Jacinta and Will, Jack and Alice telling about school. Chellie wondered what it would be like to go to school with other kids. She could hardly wait until everyone came back at Easter. As well as answering them she wrote to Mark and told him all that had happened. She also went on with Caretta's story for Miss Howe. She wrote to the turtle research people too and told them about Caretta's 117 babies. In their reply they thanked her very much. They said how pleased they had been to see the newspaper article and asked her to be one of their regular observers. Chellie was rapt.

The following week Dad went to the mainland for stores and mail. When he returned he announced, 'You've scored the most, Chellie!' and dumped two fat packets on the table in front of her.

'For me?' Chellie exclaimed, seizing them. Her new worksheets were not due from school yet, but one large envelope had the school logo on it. The other envelope, addressed to *Chelonia Green, Champion of Turtles*, was from Mark's newspaper. She ripped it open and more envelopes came tumbling out as well as a copy of *the* supplement with a note from Mark: *Thought you'd like to see this. Hope it brings results.*

Two of the envelopes had gold crests. 'This is from the Premier of Queensland!' Chellie squeaked in amazement. 'And there's one from our Member of Parliament too.'

'Careful how you open them,' Dad suggested. 'These letters are for Chelonia Green's archives.'

Mum produced a knife and Chellie slit them open.

'The Premier commends me for my actions,' she squawked, 'and our Member of Parliament does too.' She passed the letters to her parents, and picked up others which also had official envelopes. 'It's from the Great Barrier Reef Marine Park Authority! Thanking me for my responsible citizenship! And the World Wide Fund for Nature director says I'll be pleased to know they are already campaigning for clean seas to protect marine life. The Australian Conservation Foundation director says that my action helps focus public attention on the problem.

'And listen to this! James Cook University's Head of the Marine Sciences Department is pleased I want to be a marine biologist and says to contact them when I'm old enough to start the course. That's awesome!'

She pulled the last letter from its envelope. 'Oh

Mum! Dad! It's a school offering me a scholarship! The Principal says they encourage initiative and enterprise and I seem to be just the sort of student they want to help achieve her ambition.' Chellie fell silent, staring through the window out to the turquoise sea which lapped Home Beach's sticky caramel sand and ribbon of shells.

She put the letter down, declaring, 'But I couldn't go away to boarding school and leave the turtles.'

'Not yet perhaps,' Mum murmured. 'But in a year or two you might be ready,' Dad added.

Chellie nodded slowly. 'I'm like a turtle still growing inside its egg, still incubating in the warm sand of Home Beach. But the hatching time will come, and then I'll have to take to the ocean too.'

Mum and Dad hugged her.

'That's about it. But it's not time yet. Now, what about that other envelope?'

More letters came sliding out, addressed to *Chelonia Green, School of Distance Education*, with a little note from Miss Howe: *Here's your fan mail!*

Chellie blushed, then started to read the letters. Several were from students with whom she shared lessons. One wrote, *Chelonia, you're a champion!* Two were from other kids – one in New South Wales, one in Canberra – who had read the story in the paper.

There were a couple from adults, too, praising her efforts. *The rubbish may seem to go on and on. But persevere with what you've started. Never underestimate what one person's actions can achieve*, wrote an 85-year-old lady from Adelaide. A West Australian man campaigning to protect the turtles on Ningaloo Reef also urged her to keep up the good work; and a student from Western Australia sent a poem she had written when she was a volunteer at a threatened turtle colony in South America.

Chellie was overwhelmed. Caretta's death had brought all these letters to her island, all these people into her life. With so many persons caring about turtles, surely one of Caretta's babies had a chance of surviving. Chellie resolved that when she was a marine biologist she would come back with her children in thirty years time and welcome Caretta's daughter home.

Meantime there was still a job to be done. 'See ya, Mum, see ya, Dad.' Turtle Beach was calling. How many plastic bags would she find today?

You can help look after the environment,
just like Chellie. Here are some resources
to help you get started.

National Threatened Species day is held every September.

www.environment.gov.au/biodiversity/threatened/ts-day

World Wide Fund for Nature
Threatened Species Network.

http://wwf.org.au/ourwork/species/tsn

Coastcare volunteers identify local environmental problems and
work together to achieve practical solutions.

www.coastcare.com.au

Learn more about how you can help endangered turtles.

www.environment.gov.au/coasts/species/turtles/conservation.html

Clean Up Australia

www.cleanup.org.au/au/

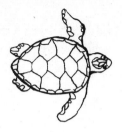

Australian Conservation Foundation

www.acfonline.org.au

The Great Barrier Reef Marine Park Authority

www.gbrmpa.gov.au

Mon Repos Conservation Park, Queensland

www.epa.qld.gov.au/projects/park/?parkid=83

Australian Marine Conservation Society

www.amcs.org.au

The Wilderness Society

www.wilderness.org.au

CHRISTOBEL MATTINGLEY has always loved the sea and its creatures. She was born at Brighton, South Australia, within sound of the sea. She lived by the beach until she was eight and loves beachcombing. Christobel also loves islands and has visited many off Australia's coast. She was enchanted by the sight of turtles swimming in the clear waters off Broome in Western Australia and has spent months in Queensland watching the turtles which come to Great Barrier Reef islands to lay their eggs. *Chelonia Green, Champion of Turtles* was inspired by visits to a special island off the Capricorn Coast, where she was shocked by the amount of jetsam from passing boats which littered the beautiful beaches. At school her headmistress taught the students not to litter, and ever since Christobel has always picked up other peoples' rubbish when walking on the beach or in the bush.

Christobel's writing career began with her love of nature and she was ten when her first pieces were published in the children's pages of the magazine *Wild Life*. Her first book, *The Picnic Dog*, was published in 1970. Her first story to be accepted, *Windmill at Magpie Creek*, runner-up for the Children's Book Council Book of the Year Award in 1972, has appeared in four editions and two translations. Her belief that one person can make a difference also shows in many of her books, as in *The Battle of the Galah Trees*, and *Lizard Log*.

Battle Order 204, the moving story of her husband David's experiences as a bomber pilot in World War 2, was published in 2007 to great acclaim. *Chelonia Green, Champion of Turtles* is the 47th book from this award-winning, well-loved author.